Louie the Lawn

Louie to the Rescue - The **Big** Dig

by Maria I. Morgan

Illustrated by Sherrie Molitor

It was Saturday morning. Louie the Lawnmower and his friends were wide awake and excited to get out into the yard.

Louie had overheard his people talking about a contest. A team of people would be voting on which home in their neighborhood would get a special award for having the best looking yard. All the lawn tools were ready to work hard so their lawn would get the prize.

The garage door opened and out walked the man and lady. Soon Louie was munching grass, and both Ruthie Rake and Bobbie Blower were cleaning up wood chips.

Next, the man carried Eddie Edger to the curb. He wheeled Eddie slowly up the driveway, making a neat, straight line. Eddie smiled when he saw the man was happy with his work.

The lawn looked great. Louie and his friends had done their best. The man and lady were pleased, but they weren't finished yet.

As the man got into the truck to go to the store, the lady picked up Henri Hose. She laid him down in a curvy pattern by the front of the house. Louie and the others wondered what was going on.

The man returned with big bushes in his truck. The people were going to plant them in the area marked by Henri Hose.

Terri Trowel was pointing to something else the man was taking out of the truck. A large silver shovel with a bright orange handle stared back at them. "What's the matter? Never seen a shovel before?" the newcomer asked.

As the man leaned the shovel against the house, it started talking again. "I'm Sherri Shovel and I do big stuff. Your people need me to dig some big holes to plant those big bushes."

With a nod in Terri's direction, Sherri laughed and said, "You're too little to do anything useful."

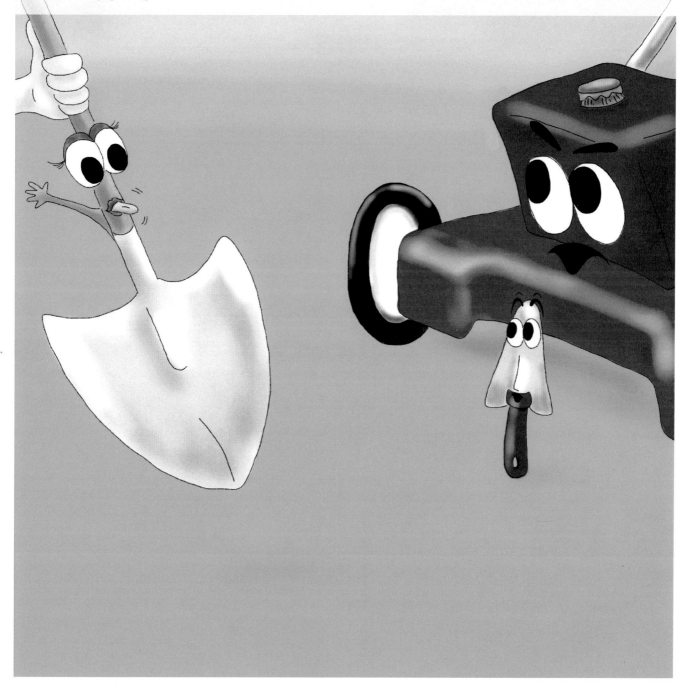

L̲ouie rolled forward. "Wait just a minute. You can't talk to Terri like that!" Sherri stuck out her tongue, but before she could say anything else, the man grabbed her by the handle and started digging the first hole.

A tear rolled down Terri's face. Ruthie put her arm around her friend. Sherri Shovel didn't even know Louie and the gang, and she was already causing problems.

When the man finished digging three big holes, he hung the new shovel on a hook in the garage. Sherri started bragging as soon as the man went inside.

"Did you see all those huge holes I dug? That dirt was tough, but I was tougher! Bet you couldn't even dig one small hole, Tiny Trowel," she challenged.

Terri spoke up with a sniff, "My name is Terri not Tiny."

Louie interrupted, "Don't pick on my friend. She hasn't done anything to you." The rest of the gang nodded in agreement.

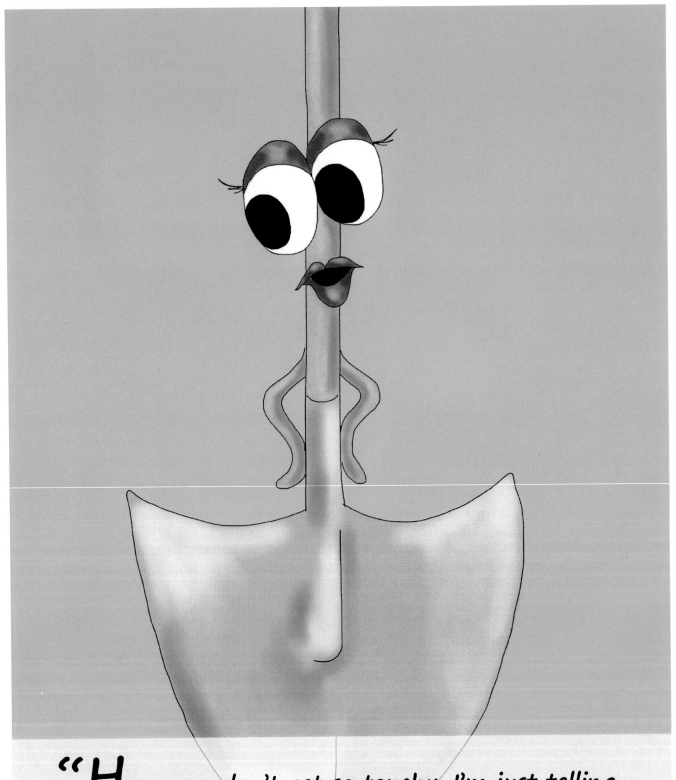

"Hey now, don't get so touchy. I'm just telling it like it is." Sherri snapped.

Moments later the lady came in to get Terri Trowel. Sherri Shovel gasped in surprise and for once she had nothing to say.

The yard tools watched as the lady used Terri Trowel to plant colorful flowers in front of the new bushes. "That's the final touch that will give us the best chance of winning the yard contest!" said the lady. The man agreed.

When Terri returned to the garage, Sherri cleared her throat. "S-sorry Terri. I-I shouldn't have said those mean things to you. I wanted you guys to like me so I tried to act tough. Instead, I made a fool of myself. We were both made to dig, and that's neat. C-can we start over?"

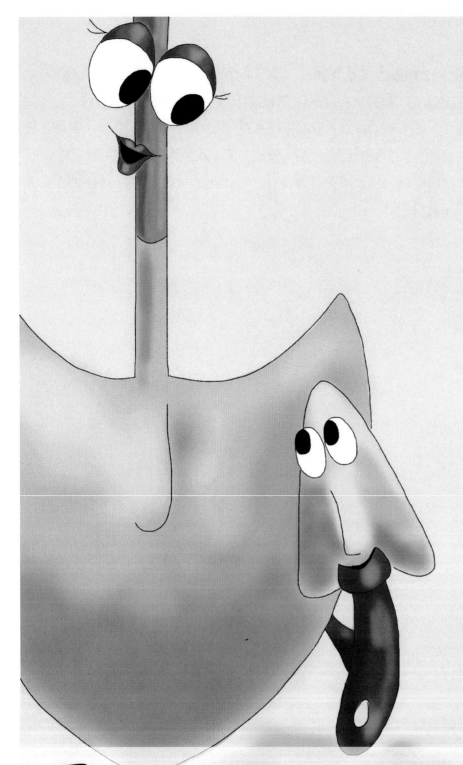

Terri spoke up, "No one's perfect, Sherri! Of course we can start over."

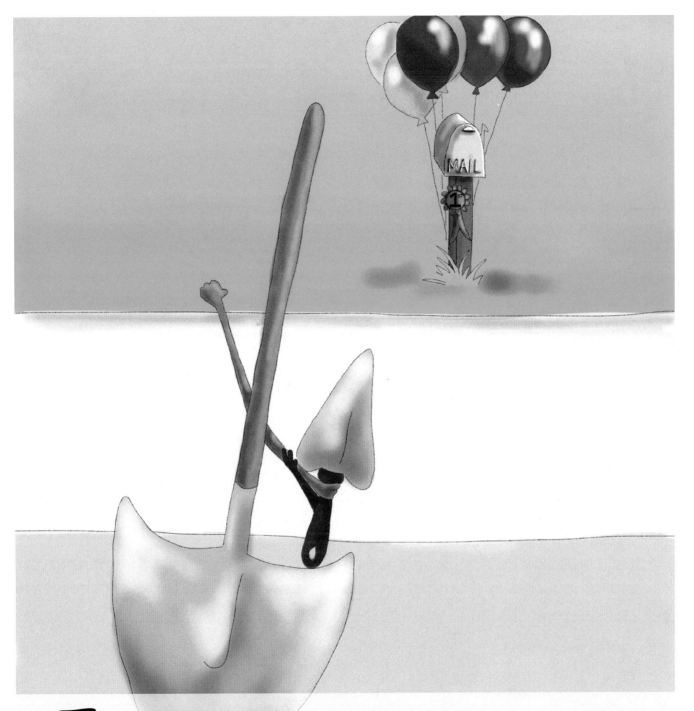

The next morning Sherri woke Terri with a shout. "You did it! The flowers you planted wowed the judges and our yard won the prize!" Sure enough, there were balloons and a blue ribbon attached to the mailbox. Everyone was thrilled.

In the quiet of the garage that night, Louie thought about the last couple days. He couldn't get over the change in Sherri. Instead of saying things that hurt the others, she was using her words to encourage them.

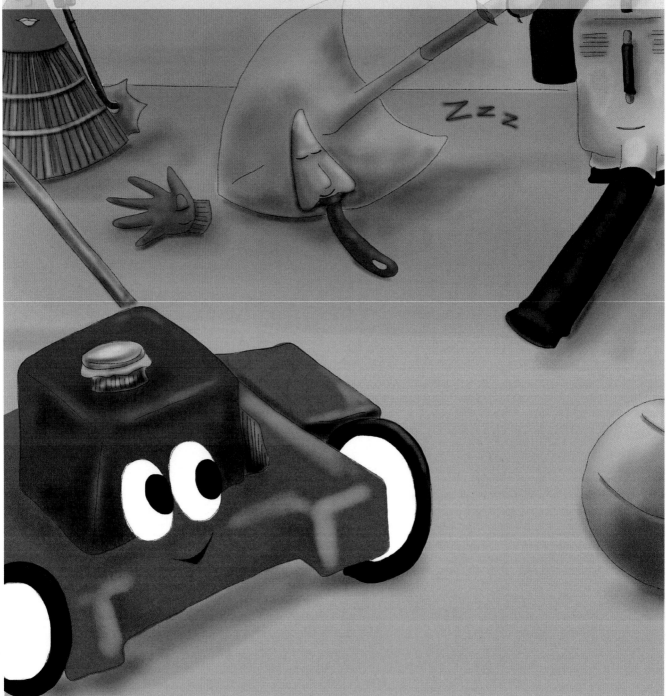

Louie's Lesson Corner:

1. My friends and I worked hard to make the lawn look extra nice for the contest. When you're given a job, do you do your best? Give an example.

*<u>Digging Deeper</u>: God wants us to do a good job and talks about it in Colossians 3:23. What does He say?

2. After the gang and I were finished working, the man and lady still had things they wanted to do in the yard. Name 2 things the man brought back from the store.

3. Sherri Shovel was a new yard tool. How did she treat my friend Terri Trowel and the rest of us? How do you treat others?

*<u>Digging Deeper</u>: God wants us to treat others with respect. Look up Genesis 1:27. How did God create us?

4. How did I respond when Sherri was rude to Terri? Do you stand by your friends no matter what?

*<u>Digging Deeper</u>: It's important to be a faithful friend. God's Word says, "A friend loveth at all times . . ." Proverbs 17:17a. How can you be a faithful friend?

After a rough start, they were all becoming friends. And that made Louie one happy lawnmower!

5. Sherri Shovel's words hurt Terri. First she bragged about all the things she could do, then she accused Terri of being too small to do anything useful. How do you use your words?

*<u>Digging Deeper</u>: The Bible has a lot to say about our words. Look up James 3:5-6; 8-10. How should we use our words?

6. The lady used Terri Trowel to dig the holes for the flowers that put the finishing touch on the yard. How did Sherri respond? What do you do when you're wrong?

7. It was important for Sherri Shovel to apologize for her behavior. Did Terri Trowel do the right thing by forgiving her?

*<u>Digging Deeper</u>: Jesus talks about forgiveness in Ephesians 4:32. Are you quick to forgive others?

8. Who won the contest for the best looking yard?

9. Following a rough start, I was happy all of us became friends. Sherri wasn't mean anymore. How did she use her words now? How will you use your words today?

Until next time,

Louie the Lawnmower

About the Author

Maria I. Morgan is an inspirational writer and speaker. She is the award-winning author of "Louie's BIG day!" Regardless of the age of her audience, her goal is the same: to share God's truth and make an eternal difference. She lives in the muggy South with her husband, two retrievers, and two Maine Coon kitties ~ the perfect mix to fuel her creativity for years to come!
www.mariaimorgan.com
www.mariaimorgan.wix.com/louie-the-lawnmower

About the Illustrator

Sherrie Molitor has been a member of both the Mid-Michigan Art Guild and the Society of Children's Book Writers and Illustrators. Her paintings have been displayed in numerous local Michigan galleries and venues. Her book illustrations generally have involved self-published authors who have wonderful stories to tell. She recently received her nursing degree and has stepped away from her career as an illustrator.

Love Louie & the gang?

Collect other books in the series:

Louie is a bright red lawnmower who used to live at the hardware store with his friends. Now he's on his own and it's time to find out if he can do the job he was made to do. Join Louie for his BIG adventure and discover the surprise that awaits him at the end of the day!

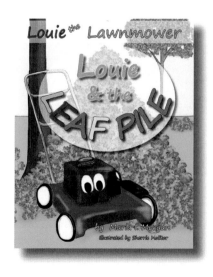

Louie the Lawnmower and his friends are back! Louie wants to be a hero and comes up with a plan to tackle a mountain of autumn leaves. Will he succeed or will he forget an important component? Join Louie and the gang in their outdoor adventure: Louie & the Leaf Pile.

Made in the USA
Middletown, DE
08 May 2020